my Purple Toes

by Blair Hahn

illustrations by Tate Nation

This book is a work of fiction. Names, characters, businesses, organizations, places, events, and incidents are either a product of the author's imagination or are used fictitiously. Any resemblance to actual persons, living or dead, events, or locales is entirely coincidental.

published by My Purple Toes, LLC

copyright ©2011 by My Purple Toes, LLC

Distributed by Emerald Book Company

ring information or special discounts for bulk purchases, please contact Emerald Book Company at PO Box 91869, Austin, TX 78709, 512.891.6100.

Illustrations by Tate Nation, tate@tatenation.com

layout and design by Atlantic Publication Group, LLC, www.atlanticpublicati

Manufactured by Shanghai iPrinting Co., Ltd. on acid-free paper
Manufactured in Shanghai, China. June 2011
Batch No. 1

ISBN: 978-0-9834778-0-8

First Edition

D1116098

We are very proud to partner with author Blair Hahn and be part of "My Purple Toes."
This is the kind of book that does more than entertain children. A significant portion of its
proceeds benefit children around the world through our charity, Soles4Souls.

We give new shoes to people in need, whether they live near you or in a refugee camp on the
other side of the world. A new pair of shoes means protection from puncture wounds, cuts,
scrapes, burns and contact with bacteria. A pair of shoes can allow access to education, as
they are often required as part of a school uniform.

The truth is the world needs shoes for its children. We receive thousands of requests to help
kids around the world (and around the corner) and we simply don't have enough to fill the
need. You can make a big difference by cleaning out your own closet!

Warm Regards,

Wayne Elsey
Founder and CEO
Soles4Souls, Inc.

Visit www.giveshoes.org to learn more, and thank you for helping us
"Change the World, One Pair at a Time!"

How did the dad in our home end up with **purple** toes?

Well, one day he went for a pedicure at the invitation of our teenage daughter.
She had seen another daddy at a nail salon with his daughter and thought it would be a grand
experience for the two of them to share. I think she was surprised dad accepted her invitation,
and she liked that he really enjoyed the experience. At the end of the pedicure, he noticed our daughter
getting her nails painted a bright pink and teasingly asked, "What about me?"
Everyone giggled and decided to call his bluff! It wasn't long before daughter and dad exited
the salon with a light-hearted pace on feet of painted toes.

— Mama Hahn

Special thanks to Clayton Woodson for blazing the painted toe trail!
I never would have gone down the path without you showing me the way.

This Book Is For

_____

From

_____

I have **purple** toes!

Purple toes are silly, **purple** toes make me smile!

This is my family.

Who else has **purple** toes?

Mama rolls her eyes at my purple toes...

Sister giggles at my **purple** toes...

Brother is embarrassed by my purple toes...

and Gus barks at my **purple** toes!

But, I like my

Purple toes are silly! Purple toes make me smile!

purple toes!

Can you count my **purple** toes?

Sometimes brother and sister sit on my **purple** toes...

and sometimes
they give me hugs!

My **purple** toes like to feel the tall green grass in the spring.
Can you find my purple toes?

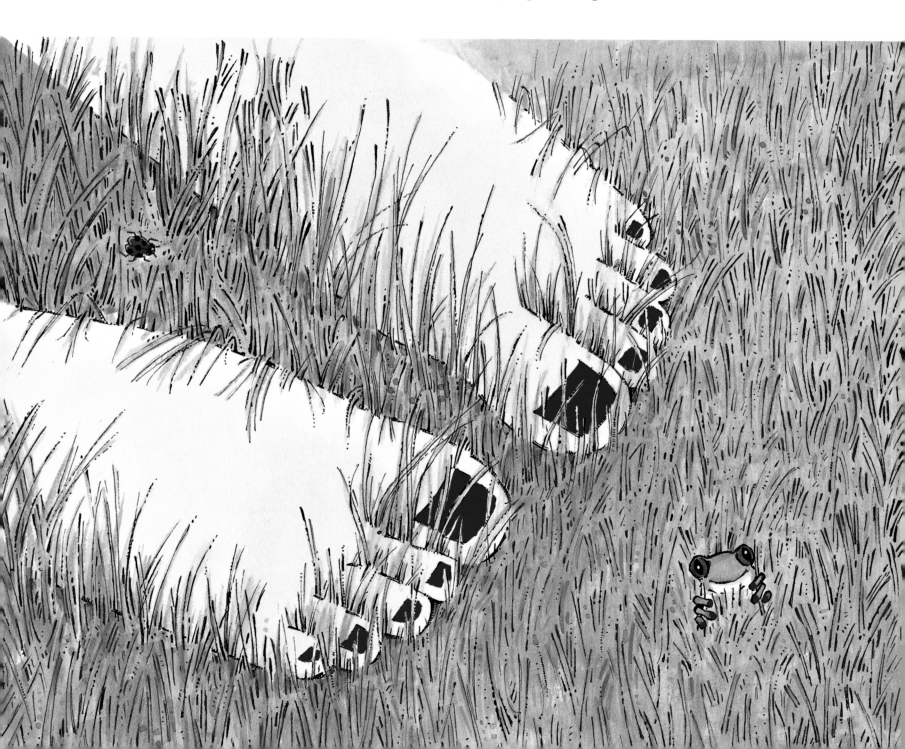

My purple toes like to play in the sand
on the beach in the summer.

Where are my purple toes?

My **purple** toes like to wiggle in the leaves in the fall!
Do you see my **purple** toes?

My purple toes like to jump in the snow in the winter –
But then they get very, very cold!

Can you find my purple toes?

And sometimes at night my **Purple** toes like to watch the fire and get warm and toasty!

Do you see my **purple** toes?

My Purple toes like to take bubble baths before I go to bed.

Where are my purple toes?

But most of all, my **purple** toes like to

Goodnight family, goodnight Gus,

be warm and cozy in my big soft bed.

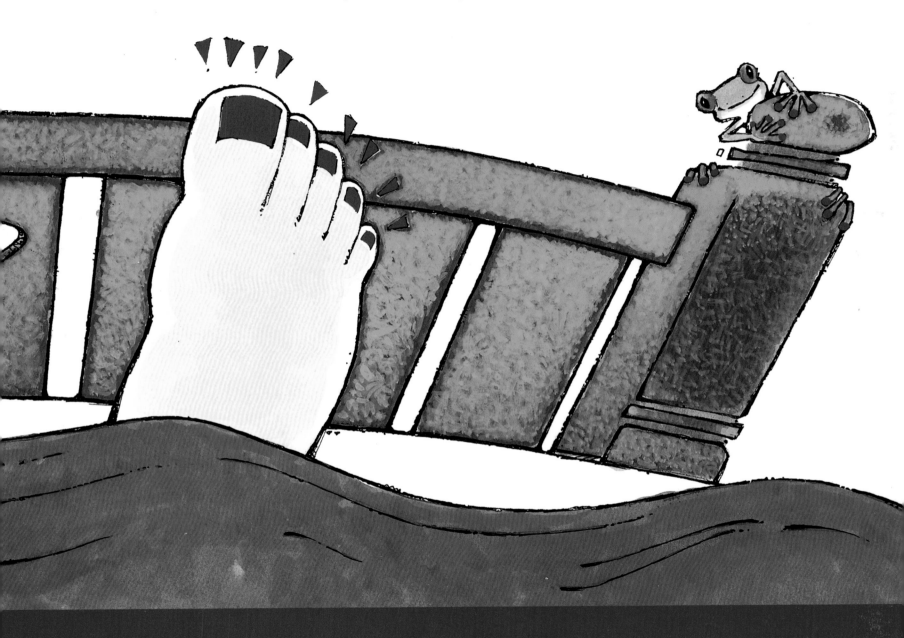

goodnight purple toes!